POKÉMON™

Psyduck Ducks Out

Adapted by Jennifer Johnson

SCHOLASTIC INC.
New York   Toronto   London   Auckland   Sydney
Mexico City   New Delhi   Hong Kong

ISBN 0-439-20091-1

12 11 10 9 8 7 6   8 9 10/0

Printed in the U.S.A.

First Scholastic printing, December 2000

The World of Pokémon

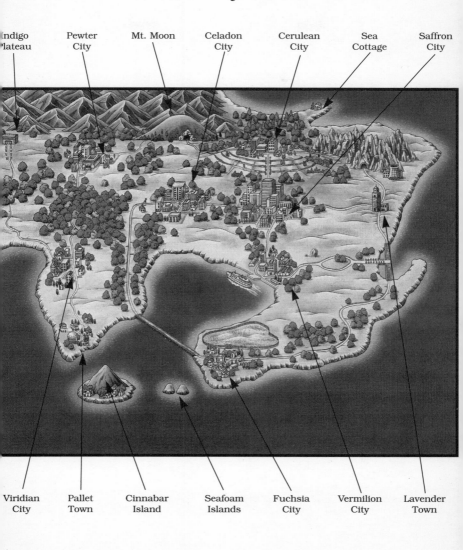

Indigo Plateau · Pewter City · Mt. Moon · Celadon City · Cerulean City · Sea Cottage · Saffron City

Viridian City · Pallet Town · Cinnabar Island · Seafoam Islands · Fuchsia City · Vermilion City · Lavender Town

Oh, Psyduck!

"This looks like the perfect place to stop and camp for the night," said Misty. She looked around. She and her friends Ash and Brock had spent the day hiking through a forest. Now they had reached a grassy clearing. A stream and some fruit trees were nearby.

"I don't know, Misty," Ash replied. "I was hoping we'd make it to the next town today. I want to battle with the town's Gym Leader for a badge."

"*Pika, pika,*" Ash's Pikachu protested.

"I guess we *could* use a rest," Ash agreed.

Misty smiled at the little yellow Pokémon. Pikachu always cheered her up. Plus, it was a great playmate for Misty's Togepi. The baby Pokémon had hatched not long ago. It was so young that the bottom half of its shell was still attached to it. Togepi loved to play with Pikachu.

Misty and her friends began to set up camp. "We're right in the middle of nowhere," Ash complained.

Misty grinned. "Don't worry, Ash. We won't be here long. Besides, we might even spot some rare Pokémon."

Misty was used to Ash's grumbling. Ash was always looking for Pokémon to capture. He hated to waste time in the middle of nowhere.

Misty knew Ash pretty well by now. She had joined him on his Pokémon journey when he was first starting out. They'd had lots of adventures so far. They'd made some new friends, like Brock and Tracey — both boys were older and gave Ash and Misty a lot of great advice about training Pokémon.

And they'd caught new Pokémon, too. Misty now had Staryu, Starmie, Goldeen, Horsea, Psyduck, and Togepi.

Ash hoped to capture all the different kinds of Pokémon in the world. He dreamed of becoming a Pokémon Master. Misty specialized in Water Pokémon. She loved the way they could float and swim and dive in the water. The way they waddled around on land was really cute, too!

"Togi! Togi!" Togepi cried. Its stomach gurgled.

"Oh, you're hungry!" Misty said. She scanned the clearing. Some juicy, ripe apples hung on the top of a tall tree. But how could she get them? Then it came to her. Her Staryu could do it. Staryu was a star-shaped Pokémon with a red gem in its center. Maybe Staryu could slice the fruit off the trees with its sharp points.

Misty reached into her backpack. She dug out a red-and-white Poké Ball. "Staryu, I choose you!" Misty called.

An orange ducklike Pokémon emerged from the Poké Ball instead of Staryu. "*Psyduck*," it croaked as it waddled toward Misty.

"Oh, Psyduck," Misty groaned, "not again!"

Ash snorted with laughter. "Gee, Misty, you're a great Pokémon trainer. You've almost taught Psyduck its own name!"

Most of Misty's Water Pokémon were smart and talented. But her Psyduck was always getting lost or confused. Misty knew Psyduck tried hard. But it could really get on her nerves sometimes.

"I don't know what I'm going to do with

4

Psyduck," Misty complained. "Sometimes I wonder why I keep it with me!"

"You and Psyduck have been through a lot together," Brock reminded Misty.

"Yeah," Ash added. "Psyduck's even helped us out of some serious trouble."

"I guess you're right," Misty said. "I'll be right back. I'm going to look for some fruit that's easier to reach."

Misty walked into the woods. Her friends' words rang in her mind. She and Psyduck *had* been through a lot together. Psyduck might be frustating at times, but it was also loyal. In fact, Misty remembered she had never actually *caught* Psyduck. The confused orange Pokemon had caught *her*. It all started when Misty, Ash, and Brock found themselves in a strange new city. . . .

2

Hypno and Drowzee

"These buildings are so tall you can hardly see any sky," Misty said as she walked downtown with Ash, Brock, and Pikachu. She thought there was something a little creepy about the city they were passing through.

"Where are we, anyway?" Ash asked.

Brock reached into his bag for a map. Brock was a Gym Leader who had put his career on hold to learn more about the habits of Pokémon. He was older than Misty and Ash and sometimes wiser — unless there were cute girls around.

"Uh . . . looks like we're in Hop-Hop-Hop Town," Brock said uncertainly.

What kind of name is that? Misty wondered.

A blue-haired police officer rode by on a scooter. Misty recognized her right away. Every town had an Officer Jenny. They were all cousins and they all looked exactly alike. This Officer Jenny had a poster in her hand. A child's face was on the poster. Jenny hung it on a wall, in a long row of posters. Each poster had a different child on it.

"What do you think those posters are for?" Ash asked Misty.

"Let's find out," Misty said.

They approached Officer Jenny.

"Who are these kids?" Ash asked.

"All of these children are missing," she replied. "They've been gone for three days. Their parents are so worried."

"That's terrible!" Misty said.

"Don't worry, Jenny," Ash told the officer. "Detective Ash Ketchum will solve this case!"

"Detective?" Misty said. "Oh, brother."
Ash had a little too much confidence sometimes.

"Where should we start looking for
clues?" Ash asked.

"Let's ask the kids at the Pokémon
Center if they know anything," Brock sug-
gested. Almost every city had a Pokémon
Center, a place you could take your
Pokémon when it was sick, hurt, or just
tired.

8

"Brilliant deduction, Brock!" shouted Ash. "Let's go!"

Misty hurried to join the two boys. Officer Jenny led them all to the Pokémon Center. Nurse Joy stood behind the front desk. They recognized the orange-haired Pokémon nurse right away. Nurse Joys were kind of like Officer Jennys — every town had one, they were all related, and they all looked alike. And, of course, Brock had a major crush on all of them.

"I'm Misty. My friends and I are here about the missing children," Misty told Joy.

"Oh, yes. All those boys and girls who disapeared. I saw it on the news," said Nurse Joy. She sighed. "I wish I could help you, but I've got my hands full with our own mystery."

"What do you mean?" Misty asked.

"All the Pokémon at the center are behaving very strangely," Nurse Joy explained. She led them to an examination room. Some Pokémon were lying on a counter there. "Just look at Cubone and Oddish," she said.

Cubone, a small Pokémon wearing a skull helmet, seemed to be in a deep sleep. Oddish, a Pokémon that looked like a weed, was sleeping, too. So were several other Pokémon lying near them.

"Even Magikarp is affected," said Nurse Joy. She lifted up a limp, fishlike Pokémon. "It's usually full of life."

Misty cringed. She hated to see a Water Pokémon in such sad shape.

"Looks like it's ready for the deli counter," Ash added.

Nurse Joy walked over to a Pokémon

with orange feathers and big, goofy eyes. "And this one's in just terrible shape," she said.

"*Psy-y, psy-y,*" moaned the Pokémon.

Misty stared at the ducklike creature. She had never seen a Pokémon like it before. She was not impressed.

"What is it?" Ash asked. Misty noticed that even Ash didn't sound very excited about the Pokémon — and he was usually excited about *any* new Pokémon. Ash took out Dexter, his Pokédex. Dexter held information about every known Pokémon. "Psyduck," Dexter said. "A Water Pokémon. Uses mysterious powers to perform many different attacks."

"Mysterious powers?" Ash asked.

"I find that hard to believe," Misty said. She turned to Nurse Joy. "So, how long has all of this been going on?" she asked.

"For three days," the nurse answered.

"Three days!" Brock exclaimed. "That's exactly how long those kids have been missing!"

Officer Jenny had an idea. "Maybe there's a connection between the children's disappearance and the Pokémon's lack of energy."

Ash looked thoughtful. "Hmmm . . . one more mystery for the mind of Ash Ketchum, master detective," he said.

Master detective? Yeah, sure, Misty thought. "Do you have any ideas yet?" She asked.

"Uh, not really," Ash confessed.

But Officer Jenny had an idea. She held

up a small device that looked sort of like a radio. "This is a sleep-wave detector," she said. "Lately I've been picking up an unusually large amount of waves that make people fall asleep."

"I'm sure they're not coming from any of the Pokémon in the center," said Nurse Joy.

"They're from outside," Officer Jenny agreed.

"*Pika . . . chu-uu.*" Pikachu was sitting on a table. Suddenly, it drooped over onto the tabletop.

"Oh, no!" Ash wailed. "Even Pikachu's losing energy."

"Hmm," Brock said. "I wonder if those sleep waves and the Pokémon's condition —"

"Yes," Officer Jenny interrupted. "They may be connected. I think we'd better find the source of those sleep waves!"

Misty looked at Ash and Brock. "Let's go!" she shouted.

3

Under Hypno's Spell

The sleep-wave detector led Misty and the others to a very weird place — a mansion on top of a skyscraper!

"The waves are coming from the mansion," Officer Jenny reported.

Brock and Ash burst through the door. Misty quickly followed them. Jenny was right behind her.

They walked into a huge room with high ceilings and plush red carpet. Men and women in fancy suits and dresses were standing around. They looked startled at the sight of Misty and her friends.

A fussy-looking man came up to them. He wore funny little glasses on a chain. "Are you new members?" he asked them.

Members of what? Misty wondered.

"We've been monitoring some sleep waves and they're coming from up here," explained Officer Jenny.

"Sleep waves," said the man. "Oh, they must be coming from this Hypno." He pointed to a big yellow Pokémon with a large, pointed nose. It was swinging a pendulum back and forth. A squatty brown-and-yellow Pokémon sat next to it. It looked sort of like an anteater.

"Hypno?" Ash asked Dexter.

"Hypno . . . a Hypnosis Pokémon," came Dexter's reply. "It carries a device like a pendulum and hypnotizes its opponents."

"And what's that next to it?" Misty wanted to know.

"Drowzee. The first Pokémon to use a combination attack like Hypnosis and Dream Eater," Dexter answered.

"I think Hypno's the evolved form of Drowzee, isn't it?" Brock asked.

The man with the glasses looked excited.

"That's correct! Our other Drowzee finally evolved into a Hypno three days ago," he told them proudly.

Now it was Officer Jenny's turn to look excited. "I knew it. That's just when those children vanished and the Pokémon started to lose all their energy."

Misty and the boys nodded their heads in agreement. "We've been using our Pokémon to help us fall asleep," said a man in a top hat.

"Who's we?" Misty asked.

"The members of the Pokémon Lovers Club!" said the man with the glasses.

"The Pokémon Lovers Club?" Misty had never heard of it.

The man explained. Everyone in the club adored Pokémon. Hypno was their favorite. The club members had something else in common, too. They all had trouble sleeping. So they used Hypno's sleep waves to help make them drowsy.

"So Hypno's sleep waves must have zapped the Pokémons' energy," Misty said.

Brock agreed. "Hypno usually uses

16

its powers only on other Pokémon," he explained. "It had to adjust its sleep waves to help humans sleep. I bet the new waves zapped all the Pokémon at the center!"

"But what about the missing kids?" Misty asked.

Just then Brock had another idea. "Maybe the wavelengths affect certain sensitive kids, too."

"Let's see," Misty said, planting herself in front of Hypno.

"*Hypno, hypno*," chanted the Pokémon. It swung its pendulum back and forth. A strange feeling came over Misty. . . .

"*Seel, seel*," Misty said in a hoarse voice. She sounded just like the white Water Pokémon. And she flapped her arms up and down like Seel, too.

"Misty, what's the matter?" Ash asked, alarmed.

"She's being controlled by the sleep wave!" Brock explained.

The gentleman from the Pokémon Lovers Club looked distressed. "We've accidentally caused a terrible situation," he said.

"*Seel, seel*." Misty ran past Ash and the others and right out of the room.

They all hurried after her.

Misty led the group into a large park. She flapped her arms and cried, "*Seel, seel*" all the way there.

Misty didn't stop until she was deep inside the park. A bunch of kids were playing next to a lake. But they weren't playing like ordinary kids. Every kid was acting just like a Pokémon.

"These are all the missing children!" announced Officer Jenny.

"Why are they acting like that?" Ash asked.

"*Pokémon-itis*," Brock explained. "Hypno's sleep waves have made the kids think they're Pokémon! Misty has it, too."

"What can we do?" Ash wondered.

The gentleman from the Pokémon Lovers Club had an idea. "What if we use Drowzee to cure the children? It gives off dream waves that may counteract Hypno's waves."

Brock nodded. "That just might work!"

The Spell Is Broken

The group returned to the mansion. They sat Misty in front of Drowzee. They asked Drowzee to focus its dream waves on her.

Waves pulsed forth from Drowzee's head. The waves floated toward Misty. "*Seel, seel,*" she said. At first, Misty kept flapping and chanting. Suddenly, she stopped. Misty looked around. She felt sort of weird. Everyone in the room was staring at her.

"Gee, Misty, you look beat," Ash told her.

What does that mean? Misty thought.

Misty didn't feel "beat." She just felt a little funny. But she was fine. "When I want your opinion, I'll ask for it!" she snapped at Ash.

Ash began to laugh. "She's back to normal," he said.

Normal? What was Ash talking about? Misty thought.

She listened to Brock and Ash talk. They planned to take Drowzee to the park. They needed them to cure all the kids who thought they were Pokémon.

Misty was starting to get it. Hypno's sleep waves must have affected her. "You mean I thought I was a Pokémon?" she asked.

"You acted just like a Seel," Ash replied.

Misty shook her head in disbelief. "That's weird," she said. "I wish I could remember it."

"I know I'll never forget it!" Ash teased.

"Come on, guys," Brock interrupted. "We have to get to the park and help those kids."

Misty and the boys grabbed Drowzee and headed back to the park. The Pokémon focused its dream waves on the missing kids. All of the kids woke up. They had no

idea what they were doing in the park. And they all wanted to go home.

"*Pika, pika.*" Pikachu was back to its old self, too.

Misty and her friends had just one stop left in Hop-Hop-Hop Town. They raced to the Pokémon Center with Drowzee in tow. Drowzee's waves cured all of the sleepy Pokémon!

Nurse Joy was very thankful. But she was still worried about that goofy Pokémon that looked like an orange duck. "All of the Pokémon are better, but this one's still holding its head."

"*Psy-y-y,*" moaned the Psyduck. Misty frowned at it. But Brock just had to butter up Nurse Joy. "Leave it to me," he told her. "Caring for Pokémon is the sole purpose of my life!"

"Then maybe you can help it," Nurse Joy said. She handed Psyduck to Brock!

"*Psyduck,*" it said. It jumped down and waddled after Brock. Suddenly, Brock didn't look so pleased with himself. Misty didn't feel too pleased with him, either.

Psyduck followed them as they walked out of town.

"Psyduck is a Water Pokémon," said Brock. "Misty, you take it!"

Misty was not interested. "Why would I want such a boring Pokémon? It can't do anything."

Dexter piped up. "Psyduck. Constantly suffers from a headache," said the Pokédex.

"Give me a break!" Misty shrieked. "This thing always has a headache?" She whirled around to look at Psyduck. Somehow she tripped and fell backward.

"My Poké Ball!" Misty shouted. One of her Poké Balls fell off belt and rolled toward Psyduck.

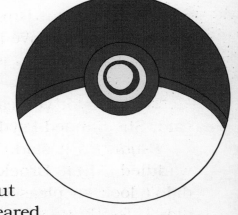

"*Psyduck*." The Psyduck peered at the Poké Ball. It pecked at the ball with its beak. The ball opened up. A beam of light shot out and Psyduck disappeared

inside the Poké Ball. "Oh, no — now it's in my Poké Ball," Misty complained.

"Good work, Misty! You caught Psyduck!" said Ash.

"Now *I've* got a headache," Misty groaned.

5

Psyduck's Mysterious Attacks

Misty wasn't crazy about her new Pokémon. Psyduck usually just got in the way. And then one day, Psyduck surprised Misty with some amazing attacks. It happened at the Fuchsia Gym, a huge, creepy mansion in the middle of a forest. The Gym Leader, Koga, was a ninja. He had lots of Poison Pokémon.

Ash battled Koga so he could earn a Soul Badge. They were in the heat of battle when the ceiling caved in!

"Team Rocket!" Misty shouted. The

Pokémon thieves, Jessie, James, and Meowth came crashing to the ground.

"Prepare for trouble," said Jessie, a teenage girl with long red hair. She wore black boots and a white jumpsuit with a red letter R on the front.

"And make it double," added James. The teenage boy had purple hair and an outfit just like Jessie's.

Jessie and James chanted Team Rocket's motto:

"To protect the world from devastation,
To unite all peoples within our nation,
To denounce the evils of truth and love
To extend our reach to the stars above.
Jessie!
James!
Team Rocket — blast off at the speed of light!
Surrender now or prepare to fight!"

"*Meowth*, that's right!" chimed in Meowth, their catlike Pokémon.

Meowth pounced in front of Koga. "Step

aside while we pick up all your pretty little poisonous Pokémon!"

Jessie and James tossed two Poké Balls into the air. Out came Arbok and Weezing!

Misty gasped. Arbok was a Poison Pokémon with some really nasty attacks. It looked like a cobra.

Weezing, also a Poison Pokémon, was a big, purple-gray ball of toxic liquids. Its attacks were just as nasty as Arbok's.

Even Koga looked worried. "We'll have to

join forces to defeat them!" he told Misty, Ash, and Brock.

"Right!" shouted Ash. He threw a Poké Ball. "Go, Charmander!"

Ash's Charmander flew at Team Rocket. The orange-red Fire Pokémon looked like a cute lizard. A fiery flame burned at the tip of its tail.

Koga's Venonat and Venomoth joined Charmander. Venonat was a furry, buglike Poison Pokémon. It had long feelers and bulging red eyes. Venomoth was its evolved form. It looked like a big lavender moth.

"Step right up!" James cackled. He made a fist and threw something at the three Pokémon.

Misty's jaw dropped. Venonat, Venomoth, and Charmander were wrapped in strands of sticky goo. The goo made it impossible for the Pokémon to attack.

"Pikachu!" Ash shouted. The lightning mouse Pokémon flew at Team Rocket.

But Jessie quickly covered it with goo, too.

Misty whipped out a Poké Ball. "We need you now, Starmie!" she shouted.

Oh, no! Instead of Starmie, Psyduck waddled out. As usual, it was holding its aching head.

"Psyduck! You're not Starmie!" Misty was desperate for a useful Pokémon.

"This time I'll choose Staryu!" She looked down. Instead of Staryu, Psyduck was still there!

Now Misty was really furious. She turned to Psyduck and shook both fists at it. "You're Psyduck — not Staryu — don't you understand?!"

Obviously, Psyduck did not. Misty turned away from it. She crossed her arms and stuck out her bottom lip. "Fine then," she told Psyduck. "Go stop Team Rocket if you want to."

"*Psy-y-y.*" Psyduck waddled up and gave Misty a big hug. That only made her more angry.

"Psyduck, you're driving me crazy!" Misty was so mad her eyes were bugging out like Venonat's. She clenched her teeth. "What attacks can Psyduck do?" she whined.

Quickly, Ash handed Misty his Pokédex. "Here, ask Dexter."

"Psyduck's Attacks. Number one: Tail Whip," Dexter informed Misty.

This better work, Misty thought. "Psyduck, Tail Whip Attack now!" she shouted.

"*Psyduck. Psyduck.*" The Pokémon wagged its tail weakly.

"How can you call that lame tail wag an attack?" Misty shrieked. She could not believe Psyduck was so completely clueless!

33

"It must have other attacks," Ash suggested.

"Psyduck's Attacks. Number two: Scratch," said Dexter.

"All right, Psyduck! Scratch Attack now." "*Psyduck. Psy-y-y-y-y!*" Psyduck raced toward Arbok. It poked Arbok with its wing. The attack did nothing to Arbok. The purple Pokémon picked up Psyduck in its fangs.

Psyduck looked at Arbok and flipped out. "*Psyduck, Psyduck, Psyduck,*" it quacked. It jumped down and ran around in circles.

Misty was humiliated. "What a totally pathetic Pokémon," she wailed.

"I think I know a way out of this!" said Koga. He pulled a cord that dangled above his head. *Whoosh!* A panel in the ceiling slid open. Dozens of Voltorb crashed to the floor.

Misty had heard about Voltorb. The strange round Pokémon looked like Poké Balls with eyes. But they were Electric and could deliver a nasty zap. Electricity crackled in the air above them.

Team Rocket stared at the gang of Voltorb. "I don't know what they are, but they're in the way!" Jessie said. She made a net with the mysterious goo. She held the net in her hand and cocked her arm. Then she flung the net at Koga's Voltorb. Dozens of Voltorb were trapped in the net!

"This is a nice little catch," Jessie cackled.

Meowth picked up a loose Voltorb. "I don't know what these things are, but I can use 'em to practice my bowling game!"

James stared at Meowth in shock. "That's a Voltorb!" he shrieked. The Voltorb on Meowth's palm rotated slowly. It opened its eyes wide. It began to glow. Suddenly, it exploded!

The blast scattered Team Rocket's goo all around the room.

Ash bent down and tried to clean off his Pokémon. But the goo seemed impossible to remove. Even Pikachu's Thundershock did not affect it.

So that explains it, thought Misty. *Most Voltorb would rather self-destruct than be*

captured. But the Voltorb in Jessie's goo net could not. The sticky stuff stopped them from blowing themselves up!

Suddenly, Meowth took a Voltorb from the net. He bowled it like a bowling ball. It rolled toward Misty and her friends.

Boom! The Voltorb exploded right in front of them. Smoke filled the room.

"Psyduck, Psyduck." When the smoke cleared, Misty saw Psyduck. It was racing back and forth in the middle of the room. Misty held out a Poké Ball. "Psyduck, return! You're going to get hurt out there!"

"What's with this loser Pokémon?" Meowth laughed.

Psyduck was in a frenzy. It paid no attention to Misty. It ran back and forth again and again. Then it fell down at Team Rocket's feet!

"Let's snatch this Pokémon, too," said James.

"We don't need Pokémon like that," replied Meowth.

Misty couldn't believe it. "Even Team Rocket doesn't want Psyduck," she said sadly.

Psyduck was back on its feet. It was racing around and holding its head again. "It looks like its headache is getting worse," Brock noticed.

Misty had had enough. "Look. You come here right now." She grabbed Psyduck.

Psyduck stood bolt upright. It stared at Team Rocket and their Pokémon. Misty could see waves from Psyduck's head traveling through the air. Psyduck was beaming them at Team Rocket!

Suddenly, Team Rocket froze in its tracks. "Wha-what's happening?" Jessie asked.

"I'm frozen! I can't move!" screamed James.

"Hey, this must be one of Psyduck's attacks!" Brock shouted.

Dexter piped up. "Psyduck's Attacks. Number three: Disable."

Then Psyduck's body began to glow with soft blue light. The light burst forward, then enveloped Team Rocket. Team Rocket and their Pokémon started swaying back and forth in a crazy way. It looked like they couldn't control themselves.

"Psyduck's Attacks. Number four: Confusion," explained Dexter.

Suddenly, Misty felt very proud. "Psyduck's attacks are pretty good," she beamed. Brock and Ash had to agree.

Team Rocket and their Pokémon whirled up toward the ceiling. *Boom!* They crashed through the roof of the mansion. Misty looked out through the hole. Team Rocket and their Pokémon got smaller and smaller as they flew away. They were blasting off again!

Misty ran to her wonderful Psyduck. "You had that kind of power all along?!" she exclaimed.

Dexter explained. "When Psyduck's headache becomes severe, it has amazing power."

"That kind of talent is a *real pain*!" Brock joked.

Koga was very impressed. "Magnificent," he boomed. "Would you like to trade that Psyduck for my Venomoth?" he asked Misty.

Misty shook her head. "I wouldn't trade my Psyduck for any Pokémon in the world."

"Misty!" Ash sounded shocked. "I thought you couldn't wait to get rid of Psyduck!"

Misty shrugged. "It's not so bad. You did a great job back there!" Misty told Psyduck. "I hope it doesn't go to your head!"

6

The Breeding Center Secret

Misty was proud of Psyduck's attacks. But she found out she couldn't always count on the confused Pokémon. Psyduck was impossible to control — or predict. There had to be some way to train Psyduck, Misty knew. But how?

Then a TV commercial gave her an idea. *"Pokémon Love Power. Find it at our Five-Star Pokémon Breeding Center,"* said the teenage girl in the commercial. She had golden hair and a big smile.

The commercial was playing on a huge

TV screen mounted on the side of a building. Misty could see it from the sunny park bench where she was sitting with Ash, Brock, and their friend, Todd Snap. Snap was a photographer. He had wavy brown hair and wore a striped T-shirt. Snap carried a camera wherever he went. He specialized in taking pictures of Pokémon.

Ash looked at the screen. "What's that?"

"Looks like somebody just opened a new Pokémon Breeding Center," said Brock.

"It's the newest thing," Snap added. "Breeding Centers raise Pokémon for kids who can't train them themselves. It's like a Pokémon spa!"

"A really excellent Pokémon Breeding Center can even help your Pokémon evolve!" Misty said.

"Let's check it out!" Ash was interested in all things related to Pokémon.

The center wasn't hard to spot. A neon POKÉMON sign flashed above its door. Hundreds of Pokémon owners swarmed outside. Misty and her friends made their way through the crowd.

The girl from the commercial was inside the center. She and her assistant stood behind a counter, checking in Pokémon. The girl was still talking about Pokémon Love Power. Dozens of kids were in line inside the Breeding Center. They all wanted to drop off their Pokémon. Misty pushed her way to the front of the line. "I've got a Pokémon, too!" she shouted.

"Misty, you're leaving a Pokémon here?" Ash looked slightly shocked.

"Yep, I'm going to try it." Misty plopped her Psyduck on the counter.

"Oh, it's so cute," gushed the girl. "Don't you just adore its eyes? They're as bright and bouncy as two Ping-Pong balls!"

"Yeah, and sometimes I wish I had a paddle," Misty muttered under her breath.

"Is there anything special you'd like us to do?" asked the girl.

Misty rubbed Psyduck's head. "There's a lot of unused space in here. And you have to change this clueless-looking face."

"That would take a miracle," Ash snorted.

The girl beamed. "Here at the Pokémon Breeding Center, our motto is, 'A little Pokémon love works miracles!'"

The girl put Psyduck on a conveyor belt.

"Bye, Psyduck. Good luck!" Misty waved as Psyduck rode off and disappeared behind a curtain.

"*Psy-y.*" Psyduck sounded even more puzzled than usual.

Misty and her friends left the Breeding Center and headed down the street. "Psyduck will prove if that place is any good," Misty told Ash, Brock, and Snap.

Ash frowned. "I bet you're just gonna

leave Psyduck there and never go back."

"No way!" Misty shouted. "I'd never abandon Psyduck like that."

"Hey, that looks tasty." Snap had spotted a place to eat. A sign above the door read RESTAURANT HUNGRY.

"Come to think of it, I'm really starving!" Misty agreed.

Ash spotted a sign in the window of the restaurant. "Look, it says 'All you can eat for free!'"

"There's gotta be a catch," Snap warned. "Like you've got to order ten dinners first."

The restaurant's chef appeared in the door. He had a kind face with a big, bushy mustache. "The buffet is free on one condition," he told the kids. "You've got to show me my favorite Pokémon!"

Misty was excited. Free food sounded good right now — especially dessert.

"I'm sure one of us has your favorite!"

Misty, Ash, and Brock showed off their Pokémon, while Snap used the opportunity to take some photos. Ash had Charmander, Bulbasaur, Squirtle, Pidgeotto, and, of course, Pikachu. Misty brought out Goldeen, Staryu, Starmie, Horsea, and her baby Pokémon, Togepi. Brock was traveling with Onyx, Geodude, Zubat, and Vulpix. The chef looked over the Pokémon. But none of them was his favorite.

Misty felt so disappointed. Then the chef pulled out a picture. "My favorite Pokémon is this one!"

Misty's jaw dropped. The chef was holding up a picture of Psyduck!

"I think Psyduck is the greatest thing since the invention of the microwave oven," said the chef. "I'm such a big fan of that spunky Orange Pokémon that whenever

customers bring in a Psyduck, I let them eat for free."

Misty knew exactly what to do. She *had* to get her Psyduck back! "Sir, if we come back in a couple of minutes, will you be here?"

"Sure. I've got to wait right here for a delivery of fifty gallons of ice cream," said the chef.

Fifty gallons of ice cream! Misty jumped for joy. "Yay, yay, yay! I'll be back in a flash!"

Misty griped all the way back to the Breeding Center. "It figures Psyduck isn't around the one time I really need it."

Ash had an annoying habit of sticking up for Psyduck. "You're the one who left it at that center!"

Back at the Breeding Center, everything was quiet. A sign hung on the front door. "Oh, no! It's already closed," Misty wailed.

Brock took the news calmly. "Guess we'll have to come back tomorrow," he shrugged.

But Misty wanted ice cream now! "I'm going to that restaurant today! There might not be any ice cream left tomorrow! Let's see if this place has a back entrance!"

At the back door, Misty banged and shouted. "Hello! Hello! Is anybody there? Will somebody please come open this door?"

Finally, Misty tried the doorknob. "It's open!"

Misty and the others slipped through the door. They found themselves in a big, empty room. "Hello? Is there anybody here who can get my Pokémon?" No one replied.

Misty tried another door. It led to a long, dark, creepy room. "Is there anyone here? It's so dark I can't see."

Brock pulled a flashlight from his bag. He snapped it on.

"What is this?" Misty shouted.

This place was no Pokémon spa! Tiny cages lined the room. The cages were crammed with sad-looking Pokémon!

Brock shone his flashlight into a cage. "Hey, here's your Psyduck," he told Misty.

Misty examined Psyduck. Its eyes looked less googly than before. "I have to admit, it does look a little smarter than when I

dropped it off," Misty said.

Brock peered at Psyduck. "Take a closer look! They just pulled its eyes back with tape!" he told Misty. He reached into the cage and peeled the tape from Psyduck's eyes.

"That's terrible!" Misty shrieked. "We've got to find out what's going on here!"

7

TWo NeW Bad Guys

"What's that?" Ash asked. A large box dropped onto a conveyor belt beside him. It was the same conveyor belt that had whisked Psyduck away.

Misty and the others followed the belt. It went through a curtain and into the lobby of the building. The girl with the golden hair was in there. So was her assistant, a blue-haired teenage boy. The boy opened the box. "Look, this Pokémon is a Sandshrew." He took out a golden-brown Ground Pokémon that looked like an armor-plated mouse.

Misty and her friends crouched behind the curtain. They eavesdropped on the girl and her assistant. The two of them didn't sound so nice anymore. "We've got a lot of Pokémon piled up in this dump!" said the boy.

"Yeah," agreed the girl. "It just goes to show that a lot of Pokémon trainers are fools."

Fools? I guess I'm one of them, Misty thought. *I can't believe I left Psyduck here!*

"Now all we have to do is pick out the choice Pokémon and ship them out to the Boss," the girl continued.

"Oh, my gosh! Those two must be Pokémon thieves," Misty whispered.

"We'll be the Boss's absolute favorites!" said the boy.

"And we'll be in for a big bonus!" the girl told him.

The boy and girl stood next to each other. "We believe in Love Power!" they shouted. "That's because we *love* power!"

"Ha-ha-ha-ha-ha!" The terrible twosome threw back their heads. They cackled with evil glee!

Misty and her friends looked at one another. "We've got to do something," Misty whispered.

"We can't let them treat Pokémon like this!" Brock agreed.

Then Snap had an idea. "I'll take pictures of this place, so everyone can see what's happening!"

"That's a great idea!" Misty said.

"Pika, pika." Even Pikachu agreed.

Misty and her friends sneaked around among the cages. Misty gave Snap directions. "Take a picture of that—there!" Snap started to take pictures.

Misty and the others tried to be very

quiet. But they didn't think that the flash on Snap's camera would attract attention.

"Is something wrong, Butch?" Misty heard the girl say.

"I thought I saw something back there," said the boy. "It looked like a flash! I'd better go check it out."

Misty and the others hid in a dark corner. They were shaking with fear.

Then Ash had a great idea. He popped Pikachu into an empty cage. *"Chu, chu."* Pikachu shook the bars of the cage. Its paws gave off little jolts of electricity.

The boy called out to the girl. "The light was only coming from a Pikachu."

He returned to the lobby.

Misty and the others sighed with relief. "I think I've got all the shots I need," said Snap.

"Good," said Brock. "Let's get out of here."

"Not without Psyduck," said Misty.

Misty ran to Psyduck's cage. She tried to free the Water Pokémon, but the cage was locked! "I can't just leave Psyduck trapped in this awful place!" Misty cried.

Misty rattled Psyduck's cage. It made an awfully loud noise.

Suddenly, a light flipped on overhead. "I knew there was something rotten going on back here!" In walked the golden-haired Pokémon thief! Her partner, Butch, was right behind her.

The girl stared at Misty and her friends. "I was right. There are *rats* in here!"

"What should we do?" asked Butch.

"Let's exterminate them!" said the girl.

Suddenly, Ash spoke up. "We're not afraid of creeps like you."

"You don't know who you're dealing with," said the girl.

"But we'll be glad to show you!" said the boy.

"Prepare for trouble and make it double," they both shouted. *Hey, that sounds like Team Rocket!* thought Misty. *I bet these two work for the same evil boss!*

The two thieves recited a crazy poem. It sounded a lot like Team Rocket's motto, only meaner!

"To infect the world with devastation,
To blight all peoples in every nation,
To denounce the goodness of truth and love
To extend our wrath to the stars above."

"Cassidy!" said the girl.
"Butch!" said the boy.
"We're Team Rocket! Circling Earth all day and night!" said the girl.
"Surrender to us now or you'll surely lose the fight!" said the boy.

A Raticate jumped out between them. "*Raticate!*" shouted the ratlike Pokémon.

The girl and boy whipped off their regular clothes. Underneath, they wore black uniforms. Their shirts had big red letter R's on the front.

So they are from Team Rocket! Misty thought. *But they don't seem as dumb as Jessie and James. They're like a leaner, meaner, and smarter Team Rocket!*

Misty felt really scared. She bolted for the nearest door. Ash, Brock, Snap, and Pikachu bolted with her. Together, they tore down a long hallway.

The new, improved Team Rocket was right behind them. "Not so fast, children," shouted Cassidy. "Now that you know our little secret, we can't let you leave!"

"We don't know any secrets," Brock lied. "We were just trying to get some free dessert!"

Butch and Cassidy weren't buying it. "You kids can't get away from us!"

Misty and the others ran as fast as they could. Misty's heart beat wildly.

She could barely catch her breath.

Suddenly, a large metal cage dropped down from the ceiling. *Clang!* Misty looked behind her. Ash, Brock, and Snap were trapped in the cage! Only Misty, Togepi, and Pikachu had escaped it.

"Misty, you'd better hide," said Ash.

"Come on, Pikachu." Misty and Pikachu scurried outside. They hid around the corner of the building. Misty watched to see what would happen.

Officer Jenny rode up on a scooter. *Thank goodness*, Misty thought.

Cassidy came out of the building. She ran up to Officer Jenny. She acted scared and upset.

"We caught burglars, Officer!" she said. "Thank goodness our security system stopped those boys before they hurt the Pokémon!"

Misty was amazed that Cassidy could sound so innocent even if she was faking.

"Don't worry, miss," said Officer Jenny. "I'll see to it those Pokémon thieves go to jail."

Misty could hardly believe her ears. Ash, Brock, and Snap were in big trouble. She and Pikachu had to get them out!

8

MiSty SaVes the Day

Think, Misty, Misty told herself. *There's got to be some way to convince Jenny that they're innocent.*

Officer Jenny had done just what she'd promised Cassidy. She had taken the boys to jail! How was Misty going to get them out?

Then she had an idea. "I've got it," she told Pikachu. "All we have to do is show Jenny some of the pictures that Snap took!"

"Pika," the lightning mouse agreed.

There was just one problem with Misty's

plan. Snap's camera was still inside the phony Pokémon Breeding Center. Misty and Pikachu would have to sneak back in and get it.

The next morning, Misty tucked her hair inside a baseball cap. She put on a jacket over her regular shorts and T-shirt. She tucked Togepi inside the jacket. Then she and Pikachu went to the Pokémon Breeding Center.

Misty felt nervous as she walked up to the counter. But her outfit worked. Cassidy didn't recognize her! And Pikachu was really short. Cassidy couldn't see it from behind the counter.

"Excuse me," Misty said to Cassidy, "I left my Psyduck here yesterday." Misty made up a story about an emergency. She told Cassidy that she really needed her Psyduck back, right away! While Misty was talking, Pikachu sneaked behind the counter. Then it sneaked into the back rooms of the Pokémon Breeding Center.

Cassidy gave Misty a big, fake smile. "I understand," she said in her phony sweet voice. She went to the back to get Misty's Psyduck.

Misty crossed her fingers. She waited for Pikachu. "I sure wish it would hurry," she said. She was afraid that Cassidy might see it. She tried to sneak toward the back to look for it.

"Miss!" Cassidy's voice startled Misty. The Pokémon thief had come back with Psyduck. But where was Pikachu? Misty would have to stall.

Then she felt a tap on her leg. Pikachu was back! And it had Snap's camera!

"Uh, thanks," Misty said quickly. "I've got to go!"

She grabbed Psyduck, and she and Pikachu ran out the door.

Misty quickly had the pictures developed, then marched into the police station. Ash, Brock, and Snap were arguing with

Officer Jenny. They were trying to tell her who the real thieves were.

Misty walked up to Officer Jenny. She handed over a fistful of photos.

"These guys are telling the truth, Officer Jenny! And I've got the photos to prove it!"

Jenny looked at Snap's photos. Each one showed a Pokémon in a tiny cage.

The officer was shocked. "This is terrible! Those two told me the Breeding Center was like a spa for Pokémon."

"That is a lie!" Misty shouted.

"They cram the Pokémon in cages!" added Snap.

Misty and the others told Officer Jenny the whole story. Officer Jenny let the boys out of jail. Then she led everyone back to the Pokémon Breeding Center.

Officer Jenny flung open the door. She shouted at the startled thieves. "So you thought you could frame these kids, when it was you who were really stealing Pokémon!"

Butch and Cassidy reacted quickly. "Raticate!" They ordered their Pokémon to attack.

"Pikachu!" shouted Ash. The lightning

mouse zapped Raticate
with its electric power.
Raticate fainted and
fell to the floor.

Butch and Cassidy
tried to run for it. But
Ash was too quick for
them. "Bulbasaur!
Vine Whip!"

The Grass Pokémon opened the plant
bulb on its back. Two vines shot out and
wrapped around Butch and Cassidy, holding the thieves tight.

Butch and Cassidy weren't going any-
where—except one place. Officer Jenny
hauled them straight to jail!

Later, Misty, Officer Jenny, and the others celebrated their victory. They finally
went to dinner at Restaurant Hungry. Misty
took Psyduck, of course. The kindly chef
was thrilled to see Psyduck. He served free
ice cream to everyone!

9

Psyduck, Lost and Found

Misty was glad she was able to rescue Psyduck from the Breeding Center. She kept Psyduck with her, even when she and Ash journeyed to the Orange Islands.

"Pika, pika, pika, pika." Pikachu ran up to Misty and Ash. They were hanging out on a sandy beach.

Their friend Tracey was with them. Tracey was an artist and a Pokémon Watcher. He was tall and had thick black hair that he always wore in a headband. Tracey loved to sketch Pokémon.

"*Pika, pika, pika, pika, pika.*" Pikachu was really worked up about something. It leaped up and down. It waved its arms in the air. Misty's baby Pokémon, Togepi, jumped around beside it. It seemed upset, too.

"What's the matter, Togepi?" Misty asked.

Tracey looked thoughtful. "Seems like something's missing, doesn't it?"

"You're right, Tracey," Ash agreed.

"Oh, no!" Misty suddenly realized what it was. "My Psyduck's gone!"

The ducklike Pokémon had been playing with Pikachu and Togepi. Now it was nowhere to be seen.

Misty, Ash, and Tracey looked everywhere. Pikachu and Togepi helped. So did all of Misty's Water Pokémon.

Tracey's Pokémon Marill and Venonat joined the search. Marill, a blue mouse Pokémon, used its large ears to listen for

Psyduck's cry. Venonat, a Bug Pokémon with big red eyes, tried to locate Psyduck with its radar. They searched and searched. But no one could find any sign of Psyduck.

Misty stood by the sea. She hung her head sadly. "Don't feel bad," Ash told her. "You did all you could. Besides, it can't be this easy to get rid of Psyduck."

"What?!" Misty couldn't believe Ash would joke about this. "Ash! We can't stop looking till we find Psyduck!"

"Well, this is a switch," said Ash. "When did you start worrying so much about Psyduck?"

"I think it's love," Tracey smirked. "I think Psyduck is secretly your favorite Pokémon!"

"No way!" Misty sneered.

Just then, a girl rowed up in a rowboat. She had spiky black bangs and a long black ponytail. "Excuse me. Are you looking for this?" she asked. The girl pointed to a Tentacruel that was swimming beside her boat. The Water Pokémon held up one octopus-like tentacle. On the tip of the tentacle

sat a weepy-looking Psyduck.

"Psyduck," Misty said, relieved

"Psy-y." The Pokémon snuggled happily against Misty's leg.

The rowboat came ashore. The girl jumped out. "My name's Marina," she said. "Your Psyduck must have fallen in the lake. I pulled it out."

Marina pointed at Psyduck's tail. Misty's eyes widened in surprise. Psyduck's tail

was glowing pink! Psyduck wagged it back and forth.

Marina explained. "I'm not sure, but from the way your Psyduck's tail is glowing, I'd say it's getting ready to evolve," she said.

"Evolve?" Ash asked, looking surprised.

"A Pokémon trainer once told me," Marina continued, "that sometimes before it evolves, a Psyduck's tail starts to glow pink, just like this."

Misty was excited. "So, are you ready to evolve?" she asked Psyduck. *"Psy-y."* As usual, Psyduck just looked clueless.

"I guess Psyduck would evolve into a Golduck," Ash said. He grabbed his Pokédex.

"Golduck, the duck Pokémon. The evolved form of Psyduck. Golduck is very adept at using its webbed hands and feet, making it the fastest swimming Pokémon of all," reported Dexter.

"Wow, Golduck sounds like a really cool Pokémon, huh, Misty?" said Ash.

Misty and Marina replied at the same time. "Golduck is one of my very favorite Pokémon," they both shouted.

Then Misty made a very exciting discovery. Marina was a Water Pokémon trainer, too!

"I just love the way Water Pokémon can float and swim and dive and surf and squirt!" Marina squealed.

"I know! I know!" Misty agreed. "Aren't they great!"

"There's just one thing I don't get," said Marina. "How come your Psyduck doesn't know how to swim?"

Misty's face turned red. She could hear

Ash and Tracey snickering. She laughed a loud, fake laugh. "My Psyduck is a rare Psyduck. But I might be willing to trade it for your Tentacruel!"

"I don't think so," Marina said. "I know. Let's have a Pokémon battle. We can see which one of us is a better trainer!"

10

Battle of the Water Trainers

"How about a three-on-three battle?" asked Marina.

"Okay!" agreed Misty. She was psyched.

Even Tracey was excited. "Wow! An all-Water Pokémon battle! I want to make some sketches of this!"

Near the shore, there were a bunch of huge boulders in the water. Misty climbed on top of one. She prepared to battle.

Marina climbed onto a boulder several yards away. She faced Misty. "I want to win this match. So I better start with something cool. I choose you, Tentacruel!"

Misty grabbed a Poké Ball. "And I'm going to start off with a Pokémon that's as good as gold. Goldeen!"

A beautiful Water Pokémon dove gracefully in the water. Goldeen had frilly fins, shimmering orange-and-white scales, and a horn in its forehead.

"Tentacruel, Wrap Attack!" Marina shouted.

Her octopus-like Pokémon swam forward, its powerful tentacles ready to strike.

"Goldeen! Use your Agility!" Misty shouted. The goldfish-like Pokémon darted from side to side. Again and again, it dodged the tentacles.

"Horn Attack now!" Misty continued. Goldeen leaped at Tentacruel. The horn on Goldeen's forehead glowed.

"I'm going to win this!" Misty shouted.

"Don't bet on it, Misty!" Marina replied. "Tentacruel, Poison Sting!" Her Pokémon lashed out.

"Goldeen, no!" Misty tried to warn her

Pokémon. Too late. The sting was too much for poor Goldeen. It landed with a splash next to Misty's rock. It was ready for a rest.

"Now I choose you, Staryu," said Misty.

Staryu flew into action. The jewel in its center glowed bright red. It shot a powerful ray of stars at Tentacruel. Tentacruel wilted. It was too tired to continue the battle.

"Now I'll call one of my strongest Pokémon," Marina said. She hurled a Poké Ball. Out popped — a Psyduck!

"Wow, that sure doesn't look like yours, Misty," Ash pointed out.

Marina's Psyduck looked fierce. It stood on a boulder. Then it flexed its wings like a body-builder. Its face looked intelligent. Its eyes weren't googly at all.

"Now I'll show you how powerful a Psyduck can be if you train it the right way!" Marina told Misty.

"Staryu, Water Gun!" shouted Misty.

Staryu took aim at Marina's Psyduck. It shot a powerful jet of water.

"Psyduck! Confusion!" Marina yelled. Her Psyduck used its Confusion Attack to repel the blast of water. Staryu was knocked down by its own blast. Now it needed a rest.

"Why don't we let our Psyduck battle each other?" Marina asked Misty.

"Our Psyduck?" No way. Marina's powerful Psyduck would cream Misty's pathetic one.

Tracey had an idea. "A battle might make your Psyduck evolve," he told Misty.

"And then Psyduck would become a Golduck!" Misty realized. "Hey, Ash, throw me Psyduck's Poké Ball."

But Ash couldn't find it in Misty's backpack. So Misty told Ash to throw the whole backpack. *Splash!* It landed in the water next to the rock Misty was standing on.

Misty sighed in frustration. She bent over and fished out the backpack. It was then that a Pokémon rose out of the water. It looked like a duck, but it wasn't round and pudgy like a Psyduck. It was tall, sleek, and elegant, with dark blue feathers. A pink gem glittered in its forehead.

"A Golduck!" Ash said. "Psyduck has evolved!"

"Wow! You're here! I can't believe you're mine!" Misty shouted. She gave the Golduck a huge hug.

"What a cutie!" Marina squealed. "I've never seen a Golduck as fine as that one!"

Misty and Marina got ready to battle. It was Golduck against Psyduck.

"Confusion Attack!" Marina shouted. Her

Psyduck used its power to create a tidal wave!

"Ride that wave!" yelled Misty. She was totally happy. Golduck *listened* to her! It glided to the top of the wave. Then it rode the wave just like a surfer.

Suddenly, the wave turned into a whirlpool. "Golduck, get out of there fast!" Misty screamed. The blue Pokémon spun around and around. It was almost sucked under.

"Psyduck, did you do that?" Marina asked her Pokémon.

The Psyduck's eyes opened wide. It shook its head no.

"What's that?!" Misty screamed. An enormous Water Pokémon, a Magikarp, rose out of the whirlpool. But it wasn't really a Magikarp. It was a submarine!

"Team Rocket!" Ash cried.

The submarine lurched out of the water. It belly flopped onto the boulders.

Misty and the others ran for it! They scrambled to safety among some palm trees.

Misty looked down. She saw that her Golduck was hopping around. She breathed a sigh of relief.

Then she saw something terrible. A big, sturdy fishing net dangled from the front of Team Rocket's submarine. Two Pokémon were trapped inside the net. Team Rocket had captured Marina's Tentacruel and Psyduck!

11

Pokémon Rescue!

"Don't you worry," Misty told Marina. "We'll get your Pokémon back."

Marina sent her Starmie to rescue the Pokémon. Misty sent Golduck to help. Golduck swam swiftly to the boulders and climbed up. It planted itself in front of the submarine. It held up one glowing finger. Then it used its Confusion Attack.

A beam of blue light shot from Golduck's finger and hit the submarine. The sub lifted up off the rocks and flew through the air. Then it crash-landed on the beach, right next to Misty and the others.

Jessie, James, and Meowth crawled out. They looked miserable. But Tentacruel and Psyduck were still trapped inside the fishing net dangling from the front of the submarine.

Marina charged toward Team Rocket. "Hey, that's my Psyduck and my Tentacruel!" she shouted.

"Just hold it right there!" Jessie warned.

"You better give back those Pokémon," Misty told them.

Jessie cackled. "You can have them — as long as you give us Pikachu!"

"Pika!" said Pikachu, looking shocked.

"There's no way you're getting Pikachu," said Ash.

"Pika, Pika." Pikachu got ready to use a Thundershock Attack. The Pokémon tensed its muscles. Its lightning-bolt tail stood upright and quivered.

"Hold it, Pikachu," said Ash. "If you attack Team Rocket, Tentacruel and Psyduck will get shocked, too!"

Team Rocket cackled with glee. "It seems

like you have no choice," said James.

"You're getting a great bargain," Jessie added. "Two for you, Pikachu!"

"Tentacruel, Psyduck!" Marina shouted, "Try to break out of that net!"

Tentacruel and Psyduck struggled lamely. But they were both tired from their battles, and were too weak to break free.

"I'll have to get them out myself!" Marina shouted. She raced toward the net.

"We can't let you do that!" Jessie threw a Poké Ball. "Arbok, go! Take care of her!"

The cobra-like Pokémon loomed over Marina. It was ready to attack. Marina screamed in terror. Suddenly, Arbok was struck by a powerful jet of water. The blast blew Arbok away from Marina.

It was Golduck! The blue Pokémon marched up behind Team Rocket!

Team Rocket spun around. "Now's our chance," said Meowth. "We've got to capture that thing!"

"Arbok! Poison Sting Attack!" yelled Jessie.

Arbok didn't have a chance. Golduck used its Hyper Beam Attack.

Powerful golden rays shot out from the jewel in Golduck's forehead. The rays blasted Arbok into the air. The purple Pokémon spun away into the sky.

Then Golduck turned its Hyper Beam Attack on Jessie, James, and Meowth. Up,

up, and away they flew! "Finally!" Ash yelled. "I was getting tired of those guys!"

Golduck lifted the net from the front of Team Rocket's submarine. It delivered Tentacruel and Psyduck to Marina. Misty raced up to her Golduck. "Oh, Golduck, you saved the Pokémon. That was totally amazing! You're the best," Misty told it.

Marina was very grateful. "Thanks, Misty! Thanks, Golduck!" she cried.

Misty and Marina had had plenty of excitement for one day. But they still had a battle to finish!

Marina sent her Starmie to face off against Misty's Golduck. The jewel in Starmie's center glowed, and a five-sided piece of glass shot out of it. The glass flew at Golduck.

Golduck didn't hesitate. It aimed a golden Hyper Beam at the glass missile. The glass exploded into a million pieces.

The explosion sent Starmie reeling back. The star-shaped Pokémon fainted!

"You did it, Misty!" Ash cried. "You won the battle!"

Marina congratulated Misty. "You're a great Water Pokémon trainer!"

"Thanks, Marina. But I'm really lucky that Psyduck evolved when it did. If it wasn't for Golduck, I think you might have won!"

Misty held out Golduck's Poké Ball. She figured that Golduck deserved a rest. The Poké Ball glowed.

"Psy-y." Out popped Misty's Psyduck. It yawned. It stretched. It held its head. It

seemed to be waking up from a long nap!

"But my Psyduck's evolved!" Misty wailed.

Just then, a group of teenage girls walked by on the beach. Golduck's eyes lit up! It raced after the girls. It leaped around and showed them its muscles.

"That Golduck isn't yours," Marina told Misty. "It just likes to show off — in front of female trainers!"

"It's just a Pokémon version of Brock," Misty moaned. Then she had a happy thought. "Maybe I'll get a Golduck anyway. You said Psyduck's glowing tail meant it was going to evolve."

Marina looked sheepish. She was obviously wrong. Misty was crushed.

"You should be happy, Misty," Marina assured her. "This proves you're a great Water Pokémon trainer. You used a wild, evolved Pokémon without even capturing it and you still won the match!"

"Yeah?" asked Misty

"Yeah!" said Marina.

Tracey and Ash agreed. Misty's feat was really impressive. There was only one problem.

"How could that battle count if it wasn't even your Psyduck?" Ash asked.

Misty gasped in horror. Then she threw a total tantrum. She held her head in her hands. She hopped up and down in frustration. "Now I have a Psyduck-sized headache!!!" she raged.

12

Psyduck Forever

Back in the woods, Misty continued thinking about Psyduck as she gathered fruit. *Psyduck and I have had many adventures together*, she mused. Of course, Psyduck had been a real nuisance some of those times. But it had also been a hero. And no matter how much it messed up, Psyduck was always completely loyal to Misty.

These thoughts were on Misty's mind as she returned to the clearing. Her arms were full of fruit. Ash and Brock had finished setting up camp and they were sitting next to the stream.

Misty sat down beside Ash.

"Hey, Misty, what's up?" Ash asked.

"Oh, I was just thinking about Psyduck," Misty replied.

"You're not still mad at Psyduck, are you?" Ash asked.

"Well, Psyduck can be annoying," Misty said. "But I guess you're right, Ash. Psyduck and I *have* been through a lot together."

"That's for sure," Ash agreed.

"Hey, Psyduck!" Misty called to the orange Pokémon. It was happily playing with Pikachu and Togepi.

"Psyduck," the Pokémon quacked.

"Do you remember when I thought you were a Golduck?"

As usual, Psyduck looked confused. It held its head. *"Psy-y-y,"* it moaned.

"I figured you wouldn't remember," Misty told it. "You were asleep in your Poké Ball practically the whole time Golduck was around.

"Psyduck." Suddenly, Psyduck seemed

to remember Golduck. It raised its wings above its head. It imitated Golduck's body-builder pose. Then it tried to strut around like Golduck did. Instead, Psyduck tripped on a rock. It fell over backward. *"Psy-y-y."*

"Oh, Psyduck!" Misty helped the Pokémon stand back up. She gave it a big hug. "You really get on my nerves sometimes. But I wouldn't trade you for anything!"

POKÉMON

GOTTA READ 'EM ALL!™

☐ BDW 0-439-13741-1 **Pokémon Movie Tie-In Novelization: Mewtwo Strikes Back** $4.99 US

☐ BDW 0-439-15986-5 **Pokémon Jr. Movie Novelization: Pikachu's Vacation** $4.50 US

☐ BDW 0-439-10659-1 **Pokémon Collector's Sticker Book** $5.99 US

☐ BDW 0-439-10397-5 **The Official Pokémon Handbook** $9.99 US

☐ BDW 0-439-15404-9 **Pokémon: Official Pokémon Deluxe Handbook** $12.99 US

☐ BDW 0-439-10464-5 **Pokémon Chapter Book #1: I Choose You!** $4.50 US

☐ BDW 0-439-10466-1 **Pokémon Chapter Book #2: Island of the Giant Pokémon** $4.50 US

☐ BDW 0-439-13550-8 **Pokémon Chapter Book #3: Attack of the Prehistoric Pokémon** $4.50 US

☐ BDW 0-439-13742-X **Pokémon Chapter Book #4: Night in the Haunted Tower** $4.50 US

☐ BDW 0-439-15418-9 **Pokémon Chapter Book #5: Team Rocket Blasts Off!** $4.50 US

☐ BDW 0-439-15421-9 **Pokémon Chapter Book #6: Charizard, Go!** $4.50

☐ BDW 0-439-15426-X **Pokémon Chapter Book #7: Splashdown in Cerulean City** $4.50

☐ BDW 0-439-15406-5 **Pokémon Pop Quiz! A Total Trivia and Test Your Knowledge Book!** $3.99

☐ BDW 0-439-15429-4 **Pokémon Chapter Book #8: Return of the Squirtle Squad** $4.50

☐ BDW 0-439-16942-9 **Pokémon Chapter Book #9: Journey to the Orange Islands** $4.50

☐ BDW 0-439-16943-7 **Pokémon Chapter Book #10: Secret of the Pink Pokémon** $4.50

☐ BDW 0-439-15405-7 **Pokémon Jr. Chapter Book #1: Surf's Up, Pikachu!** $3.99

☐ BDW 0-439-15417-0 **Pokémon Jr. Chapter Book #2: Meowth, The Big Mouth** $3.99

☐ BDW 0-439-15420-0 **Pokémon Jr. Chapter Book #3: Save Our Squirtle!** $3.99

☐ BDW 0-439-15427-8 **Pokémon Jr. Chapter Book #4: Bulbasaur's Bad Day** $3.99

Available wherever you buy books, or use this order form.

Scholastic Inc., P.O. Box 7502, Jefferson City, MO 65102

Please send me the books I have checked above. I am enclosing $_____ (please add $2.00 to cover shipping and handling). Send check or money order — no cash or C.O.D.s please.

Name _____

Address _____

City _____ State/Zip _____

Please allow four to six weeks for delivery. Offer good in the U.S. only. Sorry, mail orders are not available to residents of Canada. Prices subject to change.
POK119